*For my friends
Christine Eyre and Dorothy Kenyon
to enjoy*

Tenor Recorder Solos

*Spielbuch für Tenorblockflöte
und Klavier*

edited and arranged by
BRIAN BONSOR

© 1985 by Faber Music Ltd
First published in 1985 by Faber Music Ltd
Bloomsbury House 74–77 Great Russell Street London WC1B 3DA
Music drawn by Allan Hill
Cover design by Shirley Tucker
Printed in England by Caligraving Ltd
All rights reserved

ISBN10: 0-571-50474-4
EAN13: 978-0-571-50474-9

To buy Faber Music publications or to find out about the full range of titles available
please contact your local music retailer or Faber Music sales enquiries:

Faber Music Limited, Burnt Mill, Elizabeth Way, Harlow, CM20 2HX England
Tel: +44 (0)1279 82 89 82   Fax: +44 (0)1279 82 89 83
sales@fabermusic.com   fabermusicstore.com

Contents : Inhalt

1.	A Toye *Giles Farnaby*	page	1
2.	Bist du bei mir (If thou art near) *Johann Sebastian Bach?*		2
3.	Minuet from *Almira* (Menuett aus *Almira*) *George Frideric Handel*		3
4.	Moment musical *Franz Schubert*		4
5.	Von fremden Ländern und Menschen (About strange lands and peoples) *Robert Schumann*		5
6.	Wie Melodien (Like melodies) *Johannes Brahms*		6
7.	The sun whose rays are all ablaze (Die Sonne, deren Strahlen glänzen) *Arthur Sullivan*		7
8.	Solvejg's song (Solvejgs Lied) *Edvard Grieg*		8
9.	Tango *Isaac Albeniz*		9
10.	Après un rêve (After a dream. Nach einem Traum) *Gabriel Fauré*		10
11.	Gymnopédie *Erik Satie*		11

Preface

Practising solos cannot fail to benefit the player who listens critically to every note he plays – virtually impossible in a large ensemble – and there may well be a link between the disappointing standard of much amateur tenor playing and the instrument's almost total lack of a solo repertoire. This collection offers players a wide variety of fine music particularly suited to the tenor's characteristics, with accompaniments likely to appeal to their pianist friends.

In editing the solo part, the fact that different makes of instrument demand varying amounts of breath has been constantly borne in mind; if, at first glance, there seem to be too many breath marks, closer practical acquaintance may well prove otherwise.

Great care has also been taken to ensure that the tenor's gentle voice will not be obscured by the piano, and a sympathetic accompanist should seldom feel the need to 'play down' to balance his partner, even when the accompaniment is fairly full.

Brian Bonsor

Vorwort

Das Üben von Solostücken wird dem Spieler, der jeder Note, die er spielt, kritisch zuhört – was in einem großen Ensemble praktisch unmöglich ist – ganz gewiß nützen, und es mag durchaus einen Zusammenhang zwischen dem oftmals enttäuschenden Niveau des Tenorblockflötenspiels der Amateure und dem fast völligen Fehlen eines Repertoires von Solostücken für das Instrument geben. Diese Sammlung bietet den Spielern eine große Vielfalt an vorzüglicher Musik, die für die charakteristischen Eigenschaften der Tenorblockflöte besonders geeignet ist, mit Begleitungen, die ihren klavierspielenden Freunden wahrscheinlich zusagen werden.

Bei der Edition der Solostimme wurde niemals vergessen, daß verschiedene Instrumentenmarken verschieden viel Atem benötigen; wenn, auf den ersten Blick, zu viele Atemzeichen vorhanden zu sein scheinen, so mag sich aus einer näheren praktischen Kenntnis sehr wohl ein anderes Urteil ergeben.

Viel Mühe wurde auch darauf verwendet, sicherzustellen, daß die sanfte Stimme der Tenorblockflöte nicht durch das Klavier in den Hintergrund gedrängt wird, und ein einfühlsamer Begleiter sollte selten die Notwendigkeit verspüren, gedämpft zu spielen, um mit seinem Partner im Gleichgewicht zu sein, sogar dann nicht, wenn die Begleitung etwas voller ist.

Brian Bonsor

Deutsche Übersetzung: Dorothee Eberhardt

1. A TOYE

G. FARNABY
(c. 1563 – 1640)

From *The Fitzwilliam Virginal Book* (II/270), compiled early in the 17th century but unpublished until late in the 19th. In the original version, this piece appears with note-values as here but in 4/2 time. A repeat of bars 9–16 in the original is omitted in this arrangement.

Aus *The Fitzwilliam Virginal Book* (II/270), das zu Anfang des 17. Jahrhunderts zusammengetragen wurde, jedoch bis ins späte 19. Jahrhundert unveröffentlicht blieb. In der Originalversion erscheint dieses Stück mit denselben Notenwerten wie hier, jedoch mit der Taktangabe von 4/2. Weiterhin sind die Takte 9–16 im Original wiederholt, während sie in diesem Arrangement ausgelassen wurden.

© 1985 by Faber Music Ltd.

This music is copyright. Photocopying is illegal.

2. BIST DU BEI MIR
If thou art near

J.S. BACH?
(1685 – 1750)

From the *Clavierbüchlein vor Anna Magdalena Bach* (1722–25), formerly believed to have been written by Bach for his wife Anna Magdalena but now thought to be by another hand, possibly that of G.H. Stölzel (1690–1749), a German composer whose work Bach admired, copied and performed.

Aus dem *Clavierbüchlein vor Anna Magdalena Bach* (1722–25), von dem man früher annahm, Bach habe es für seine Frau Anna Magdalena geschrieben, jetzt jedoch meint, daß es von anderer Hand stammt, möglicherweise der G.H. Stölzels (1690–1749), eines deutschen Komponisten, dessen Werk Bach bewunderte, kopierte und aufführte.

3. MINUET FROM 'ALMIRA'
Menuett aus 'Almira'

G.F. HANDEL
(1685–1759)

Almira, Handel's first opera, was a great success when it was produced in Hamburg in 1705. This Minuet by the 19-year-old composer is already typical of those that were to pour from his pen in later years.

Almira, Händels erste Oper, war ein großer Erfolg, als sie im Jahre 1705 in Hamburg aufgeführt wurde. Dieses Menuett des neunzehnjährigen Komponisten ist bereits typisch für die, die in späteren Jahren von seiner Feder fließen sollten.

4. MOMENT MUSICAL

F. SCHUBERT
(1797–1828)

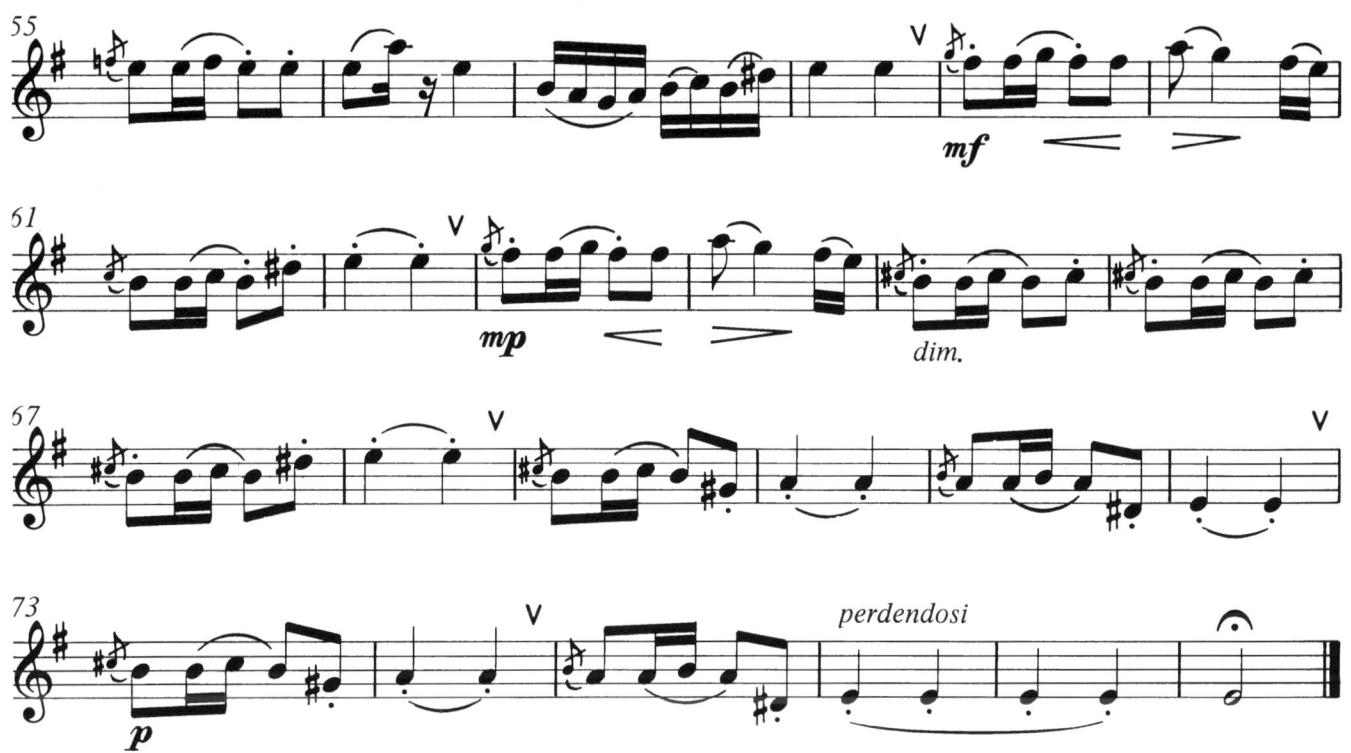

The third of the four *Moments Musicaux* for piano, op.94 (D.780), first published in 1828, the year of Schubert's death.

Das dritte der vier *Moments Musicaux* für Klavier, op.94 (D.780), erstmals erschienen im Jahre 1828, Schuberts Todesjahr.

5. VON FREMDEN LÄNDERN UND MENSCHEN
About strange lands and peoples

R. SCHUMANN
(1810–1856)

The first of the *Kinderszenen* (Scenes from childhood) for piano, op.15, composed in 1838.

Die erste der *Kinderszenen* für Klavier, op.15, komponiert im Jahre 1838.

6. WIE MELODIEN
Like melodies

J. BRAHMS
(1833 – 1897)

No. 1 of the *Fünf Lieder*, op. 105. Brahms wrote this lovely song in 1886, at the height of his powers.

Nr. 1 der *Fünf Lieder* op. 105. Brahms schrieb dieses liebliche Lied im Jahre 1886, auf der Höhe seiner Schaffenskraft.

7. THE SUN WHOSE RAYS ARE ALL ABLAZE
Die Sonne, deren Strahlen glänzen

A. SULLIVAN
(1842 – 1900)

From Act 2 of *The Mikado*, first produced at the Savoy Theatre, London in 1885. Try to read Gilbert's brilliant words; they will help you to group the semiquavers correctly.

Aus dem 2. Akt von *The Mikado*, das im Jahre 1885 im Savoy Theater, London uraufgeführt wurde. Versuche, Gilberts geistreiche Worte zu lesen; sie werden dir dabei helfen, die Sechzehntel richtig zu gruppieren.

8. SOLVEJG'S SONG
Solvejgs Lied

E. GRIEG
(1843 – 1907)

From the incidental music to Ibsen's *Peer Gynt*, the composition of which occupied Grieg from 1874 to 1875. Try the fingering for the last note of the piece; blow *very* gently – and *listen*!

Aus der Bühnenmusik zu Ibsens *Peer Gynt*, deren Komposition Grieg von 1874 bis 1875 in Anspruch nahm. Probiere für die letzte Note des Stückes diesen Fingersatz aus; blase *sehr sanft* – und *höre dir zu*!

9. TANGO

I. ALBENIZ (1860–1909)

From *España*, op. 165, a set of six pieces for piano written in 1890. This is a useful study in enharmonic equivalents! Remember that E♯ = F♮, A♯ = B♭, and B♯ = C♮ and you will find that it is not nearly as difficult as it may at first appear. The following fingerings may also be helpful; to play the ornaments, raise and lower the fingers marked by arrows:

Aus *España* op. 165, einer Serie von sechs Stücken für Klavier, geschrieben im Jahre 1890. Dieses Stück ist eine nützliche Übung für enharmonische Verwechslungen! Denke daran, daß Eis=F, Ais=B und His=C, dann wirst du sehen, daß es nicht annähernd so schwierig ist, wie es anfangs erscheinen mag. Die folgenden Fingersätze könnten ebenfalls von Nutzen sein; hebe und senke zum Spielen der Ornamente die durch Pfeile bezeichneten Finger:

10. APRÈS UN RÊVE
After a dream. (Nach einem Traum)

G. FAURÉ
(1845 – 1924)

This song, first published in 1878, is far too beautiful to be left exclusively to singers! The long phrases are, however, a real test of your breath-control, and deep diaphragmatic breathing is essential. Make sure that you lift the lower ribs *and not your shoulders*. VV signifies a particularly deep breath.

Dieses Lied, das erstmals im Jahre 1878 veröffentlicht wurde, ist viel zu schön, um ganz den Sängern überlassen zu werden! Die langen Phrasen sind jedoch ein echter Test für deine Atemkontrolle, und tiefes Atmen vom Zwerchfell ist wesentlich. Sei dir sicher, daß du die unteren Rippen anhebst *und nicht die Schultern*. VV ist das Zeichen für ein besonders tiefes Atemholen.

11. GYMNOPÉDIE

E. SATIE
(1866 – 1925)

No. 1 of *Trois Gymnopédies* (1888). The Gymnopaidiai were an ancient Spartan festival, including choral performances as well as athletic contests. This piece is another searching test of your breath-control. Play the melody line as smoothly as possible, using the softest tonguings that you can.

Nr. 1 der *Trois Gymnopédies* (1888). Die Gymnopaidiai waren Festspiele im alten Sparta, die sowohl Chorarbeitungen als auch athletische Wettkämpfe umfassten. Dieses Stück ist eine weitere eingehende Prüfung deiner Atemkontrolle. Spiele die Melodielinie so flüssig wie möglich, und verwende gleichzeitig den sanftesten Zungenanstoß, den du zur Verfügung hast.

RECORDER MUSIC
from Faber Music

SALLY ADAMS
First Repertoire for Descant Recorder
ISBN 0-571-52328-5

BRIAN BONSOR
Play Country Dances
ISBN 0-571-51004-3

The Really Easy Recorder Book
ISBN 0-571-51037-X

PAUL HARRIS
Improve your sight-reading! Descant Recorder Grades 1–3
ISBN 0-571-51373-5

MARLENE HOBSBAWM
Me and My Recorder Part 1
ISBN 0-571-51045-0

Me and My Recorder Part 2
ISBN 0-571-51052-3

PAM WEDGWOOD
Really Easy Jazzin' About for recorder
ISBN 0-571-52408-7

Easy Jazzin' About for recorder
ISBN 0-571-52329-3

RecorderWorld pupil's book 1
ISBN 0-571-51985-7

RecorderWorld pupil's book 2
ISBN 0571-52239-4

SALLY ADAMS AND PAUL HARRIS
50 Graded Studies for recorder
ISBN 0-571-52318-8

fabermusic.com

ISBN10: 0-571-50474-4
EAN13: 978-0-571-50474-9